The Quest for Aztec Gold:
MEXICO

BOOK ⑩

D0954007

Join Secret Agent Jack Stalwart on his other adventures:

The Escape of the Deadly Dinosaur:
USA
Book ①

The Search for the Sunken Treasure:
AUSTRALIA
Book ②

The Mystery of the Mona Lisa:
FRANCE
Book ③

The Caper of the Crown Jewels:
ENGLAND
Book ④

The Secret of the Sacred Temple:
CAMBODIA
Book ⑤

The Pursuit of the Ivory Poachers:
KENYA
Book ⑥

The Puzzle of the Missing Panda:
CHINA
Book ⑦

Peril at the Grand Prix:
ITALY
Book ⑧

The Deadly Race to Space:
RUSSIA
Book ⑨

The Quest for Aztec Gold: MEXICO

Elizabeth Singer Hunt

Illustrated by Brian Williamson

WEINSTEIN BOOKS

ISBN: 978-1-60286-079-7

First Edition
16   15   14   13   12   11   10   9

For Elizabeth and Felicity

Destination:
MEXICO

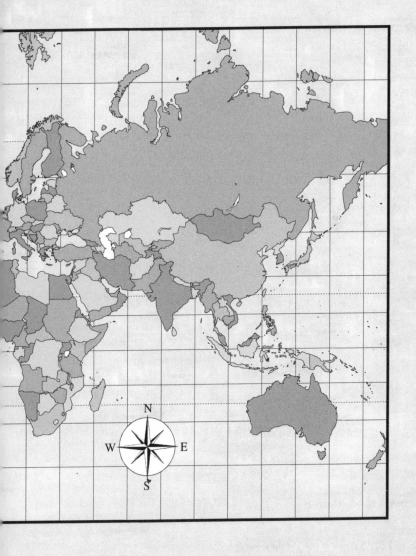

JACK STALWART

Jack Stalwart applied to be a secret
agent for the Global Protection
Force four months ago.

My name is Jack Stalwart. My older brother,

Max, was a secret agent for you, until he

disappeared on one of your missions. Now I

want to be a secret agent too. If you choose

me, I will be an excellent secret agent and get

rid of evil villains, just like my brother did.

Sincerely,

Jack Stalwart

THINGS YOU'LL FIND IN EVERY BOOK

Watch Phone: The only gadget Jack wears all the time, even when he's not on official business. His Watch Phone is the central gadget that makes most others work. There are lots of important features, most importantly the "C" button, which reveals the code of the day—necessary to unlock Jack's Secret Agent Book Bag. There are buttons on both sides, one of which ejects his life-saving Melting Ink Pen. Beyond these functions, it also works as a phone and, of course, gives Jack the time of day.

Global Protection Force (GPF): The GPF is the organization Jack works for. It's a worldwide force of young secret agents whose aim is to protect the world's people, places and possessions. No one knows exactly where its main offices are located (all correspondence and gadgets for repair are sent to a special PO Box, and training is held at various locations around the world), but Jack thinks it's somewhere cold, like the Arctic Circle.

Whizzy: Jack's magical miniature globe. Almost every night at precisely 7:30 P.M., the GPF uses Whizzy to send Jack the identity of the country that he must travel to. Whizzy can't talk, but he can cough up messages. Jack's parents don't know Whizzy is anything more than a normal globe.

The Magic Map: The magical map hanging on Jack's bedroom wall. Unlike most maps, the GPF's map is made of a mysterious wood. Once Jack inserts the country piece from Whizzy, the map swallows Jack whole and sends him away on his missions. When he returns, he arrives precisely one minute after he left.

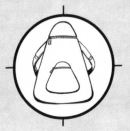

Secret Agent Book Bag: The Book Bag that Jack wears on every adventure. Licensed only to GPF secret agents, it contains top-secret gadgets necessary to foil bad guys and escape certain death. To activate the bag before each mission, Jack must punch in a secret code given to him by his Watch Phone. Once he's away, all he has to do is place his finger on the zipper, which identifies him as the owner of the bag and immediately opens.

THE STALWART FAMILY

Jack's dad, John

He moved the family to England when Jack was two, in order to take a job with an aerospace company. Jack's dad thinks he is an ordinary boy and that his other son, Max, attends a school in Switzerland. Jack's dad is American and his mum is British, which makes Jack a bit of both.

Jack's mum, Corinne

One of the greatest mums as far as Jack is concerned. When she and her husband received a letter from a posh school in Switzerland inviting Max to attend, they were overjoyed. Since Max left six months ago, they have received numerous notes in Max's handwriting telling them he's OK. Little do they know it's all a lie and that it's the GPF sending those letters.

Jack's older brother, Max

Two years ago, at the age of nine, Max joined the GPF. Max used to tell Jack about his adventures and show him how to work his secret-agent gadgets. When the family received a letter inviting Max to attend a school in Europe, Jack figured it was to do with the GPF. Max told him he was right, but that he couldn't tell Jack anything about why he was going away.

Nine-year-old Jack Stalwart

Four months ago, Jack received an anonymous note saying: "Your brother is in danger. Only you can save him." As soon as he could, Jack applied to be a secret agent too. Since that time, he's battled some of the world's most dangerous villains, and hopes some day in his travels to find and rescue his brother, Max.

DESTINATION:
Mexico

The north of Mexico has deserts, the south has many jungles.

❑

Mexico is the world's largest Spanish-speaking country.

❑

The capital city of Mexico is Mexico City.

❑

It is on the continent of North America.

❑

Mexico's currency is the Peso.

More than 100 million people live there.

THE AZTEC CIVILIZATION: FACTS AND FIGURES

The word "Aztec" is used to describe an ancient people who shared customs and spoke the Nahuatl language.

The Aztecs ate mainly corn, beans, chillis and tomatoes. They also ate grasshoppers and ants!

Their capital city was called Tenochtitlán (pronounced Te-noch-tit-lan), which was destroyed by the Spanish in 1521.

In 1978, Tenochtitlán was rediscovered by some electricity workers who stumbled upon a stone carving and started excavating.

GPF Fact File:
Hernán Cortés and the Spanish

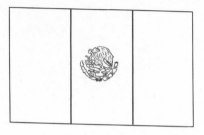

Hernán Cortés was part of a
group of Spanish "conquistadores"
who took control of lands
on behalf of their
Emperor Charles V.

In 1519, Cortes landed on present-day
Mexico and began to march
with his men toward
Tenochtitlán.

After tricking the ruler of the Aztecs,
Montezuma II, Cortés imprisoned
and killed him.

After that, the Spanish took over.
All but 5 percent of the original Aztecs
died from fighting and smallpox,
a disease the Spanish brought
to Mexico.

Cortés ruled Mexico until 1524.

Mexico received its independence
from Spain three centuries later,
in 1821.

AZTEC SYMBOLS

SECRET AGENT GADGET INSTRUCTION MANUAL

 **Double A Device:** If you're looking for information on or the location of an ancient site, use the GPF's Double A Device. Just type in what you know (key words or phrases) and this handheld gadget will try to help you out. Great for getting clues on the whereabouts of a lost city or for mapping current archaeological digs.

 **Abseil Kit:** When there's no other way down a mountain or rock face, use the GPF's Abseil Kit. The kit includes ropes, a harness and an abseil anchor. You will also need your Noggin Mold. Attempt to descend only if you've attended Mr. Kennedy's abseil training class.

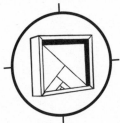

Portable Map: Small

enough to fit in your Book Bag, this wooden square opens up to the size of your Magic Map. Just place the jigsaw piece inside as normal and it will transport you home or to your next mission.

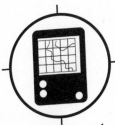

Map Mate: When you're lost

or need to get somewhere fast, use the GPF's Map Mate. This clever gadget receives signals from satellites in space to give you a map of any country, city or town in the world. It can also show you how to get from one place to another using directional arrows to guide the way.

Chapter 1:
The Chase

Secret Agent Jack Stalwart was running for his life. He was sprinting across an open plain, trying to escape from four dark shadows that were chasing him at top speed.

Jack spied a prickly bush up ahead. Rather than run around it, he jumped right over.

BLAM!

His feet crashed to the ground, spraying sandy dust into the air.

BLAM! BLAM! BLAM! BLAM!

The shadows jumped too, grunting as they landed. It felt as though they were close enough to almost touch Jack. But he was still a few seconds ahead.

Reaching for his Book Bag, he tried to grab one of his life-saving gadgets. But Jack's Book Bag wasn't on his back. Strange, he thought. It was always there.

Out of nowhere, Jack stumbled. He fell forward, his hands slamming into the sand. He rolled over several times and tried to get himself upright. But the shadows soon reached him, howling with evil laughter.

"Noooo!" Jack screamed, as the dark figures leaned over and . . .

Chapter 2:
The Hunter

"Noooo!" Jack yelled again, and sat bolt upright in his bed at home. He was sweating and shaking. Confused, Jack looked around.

It was definitely his bedroom. Whizzy was asleep on his bedside table. The clock next to Whizzy said 7:15 P.M., and Jack's Magic Map was still on his wall. What had seemed like a real life-or-death chase was nothing more than a bad dream.

Feeling something leaning against his stomach, he reached down to pick it up. It was a book called *The Most Dangerous Treasure Hunters in the World*. That would explain the nightmare, he thought. Jack had dozed off before his normal bedtime while reading about the adventures of the notorious treasure hunter, Callous Carl.

Callous Carl ruled the southern part of America when it came to treasure hunting. If there was gold to find, Callous Carl and his gang of bandits weren't too far behind.

He had been given the name "Callous" because he was heartless and because years of digging up gold had turned his hands rough, like sandpaper. Although nobody knew exactly how many men worked for Carl, there were estimates he had up to ten men in his gang.

The book had a description of the chief outlaw.

Carl was missing a right eyebrow, and he wore beat-up cowboy clothes and red leather boots. He carried a pointed dagger in a sheath on his hip. Callous Carl definitely belonged in Jack's book. He was one dangerous dude.

"Are you okay?" said a voice, as a knock came from the other side of Jack's door. It was Jack's mother. She must have heard him shout out. She opened the door a crack, and stuck her face around it.

"I'm okay, Mum," said Jack, holding up his book. "I fell asleep while reading this, and I guess it gave me a nightmare."

"Glad you're all right," she said. "Just make sure to get yourself ready for bed. It's almost seven thirty. Love you," she added, as she blew him a kiss and closed the door.

Chapter 3:
The Setting

With the fright of the dream, Jack had forgotten the time. It was almost 7:30 P.M., and he was about to find out whether he was off on a mission tonight.

Although his parents and friends thought he was an ordinary boy, Jack was actually a secret agent. He worked for the Global Protection Force, or GPF, an organization whose role was to protect the world's most precious treasures.

Whether it was stopping a thug from stealing the Rosetta Stone, or an animal trafficker from selling endangered species, nothing was too difficult for a GPF agent.

In the four short months since Jack was sworn in, he'd stopped no less than twelve evil criminals. That's why the GPF gave him the code name "Courage," which, not coincidentally, was also the meaning of his surname, "Stalwart."

As the clock changed over to 7:30 P.M., Whizzy, Jack's GPF globe, began to twirl. As Whizzy spun around and around, Jack watched him reach top speed. Whizzy coughed—Ahem!—and a jigsaw piece flew out of his mouth.

This one was large, thought Jack, as he recognized its shape. Rushing over, Jack picked it up and carried it to the Magic Map on his wall. Placing it to the south of the USA, Jack slipped the piece in and stepped back. The name MEXICO appeared in the middle of the country and then disappeared.

He wondered what was going wrong in that country. Perhaps there was something amiss at the Zócalo, the main square in Mexico City. Or maybe there was danger on the beaches of Cancún.

Knowing there wasn't much time, Jack hurried over to his bed. He knelt down and lifted up his bedsheets. Spying his GPF Book Bag underneath, he pulled it out, and asked his Watch Phone for the code of the day.

When it played back FIESTA, he keyed it into the lock on his Book Bag, and instantly, the lock popped open. Rummaging through, he noticed the Flyboard was there, as was the Map Mate. There were also some new gadgets in there, like the Double-A Device and the Abseil Kit. Jack had read about them in the *GPF Electronic News* and was anxious to see whether he could use them on his upcoming mission.

Putting everything away, he tossed his Book Bag over his shoulders and ran back in front of the Magic Map. As the white light grew from inside the country, he waited until the time was right. When it was, he yelled "Off to Mexico!" The brilliant light exploded and swallowed Jack into the Magic Map.

Chapter 4:
The Assignment

When Jack arrived in Mexico, he found himself in the middle of a dry and dusty terrain. There was hard earth under his feet, and scrubby bushes dotted the plains. Since he knew that a lot of southern Mexico was covered in rain forest, he figured he was somewhere between the middle and the north of the country.

Up ahead, he could see a collection of

one-story wooden houses. Thinking that
whoever had called the GPF was in one of
them, he made his way for the closest
one. As he approached the house, he
looked through the window and noticed
there was someone inside. From what
Jack could tell it was an elderly Mexican
man. The man was sitting in a rocking
chair in his den. When he spied Jack, he
waved furiously for him to come in.

Thinking this was his contact, Jack
walked to the front door. Rather than just
open it, he knocked, to be polite.

"*Habla inglés?*" Jack called out,
checking whether the man spoke English.

"Yes," said the voice inside. "Come
in . . . come in!"

Jack turned the handle and pushed the
door open. He found himself standing in
a cozy, tidy house.

"Come in," the man said again, telling Jack to join him in the den. Jack made himself comfortable in a squishy brown leather chair.

The old man was tall and thin, and had wavy white hair and a thick bushy mustache. Jack guessed his age was about seventy.

"The name is José Garcia," he said, holding out his right hand toward Jack.

Jack put out his hand too and introduced himself. When the two had finished their greeting, the man got up as if he were headed off somewhere. "*Café*

con leche?" he asked. He wanted to make Jack something to drink.

"No thanks," said Jack. He didn't want to be rude, but while some kids at home were allowed to drink coffee with milk, he didn't like it much.

"So," said the man, sitting back down. "Shall I tell you why I called the GPF?"

"Yes," said Jack, anxious to hear about his mission. He wondered what on earth this old man could need from the GPF organization.

"Someone has stolen something from me," the man said. "Something more than five hundred years old." This grabbed Jack's attention. Anything that old was classified as an antique. Whatever it was, it was worthy of full GPF protection.

"What is it?" asked Jack.

"A map," replied Mr. Garcia. "The lost map of Montezuma's gold."

Chapter 5:
The First Clue

Jack nearly fell off his chair. If what the man was saying was true, then this was a very special mission indeed. Montezuma II was the ancient ruler of the Aztec people, who lived on the land between Mexico and Honduras from the fourteenth to the sixteenth century.

In 1519, the Spanish landed on the coast of Mexico and marched to the Aztec city of Tenochtitlán. They conquered it, making sure that Montezuma was killed in the process.

There were rumors that before the Spanish arrived, Montezuma had his men hide much of his wealth. While the Spanish made off with whatever they could find in the city, the whereabouts of this gold had tempted treasure hunters for years.

"Where did you get the map?" asked Jack. He was a bit suspicious. A map as legendary as this would not normally be sitting in some old guy's house in the middle of Mexico.

"My good friend, Carlos Ortega, is a renowned archaeologist. Ever heard of him?" Mr. Garcia asked, raising his eyebrows at Jack.

Unfortunately, he hadn't. Jack shook his head.

"Well," the man explained, "he was one

of the principal archaeologists at the dig at Tenochtitlán."

Jack had heard something about this in Mrs. Butterworth's GPF archaeology tutorial. In the 1970s, an electricity worker discovered a precious Aztec stone. Scientists did some digging around that stone and unearthed the ancient Aztec city of Tenochtitlán, buried under present-day Mexico City.

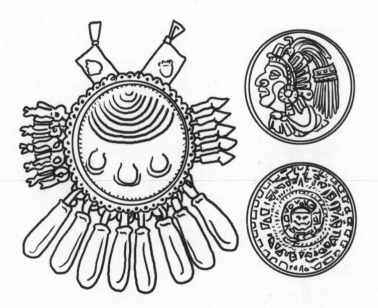

Since then, archaeologists had been excavating it bit by bit. Recently, they'd found the Templo Mayor, where Aztec priests performed human sacrifices.

"Ortega found the treasure map on a scroll hidden in one of the walls of the palace," Mr. Garcia explained, "and gave it to me to watch."

"Why you?" asked Jack.

"Because I'm a trustworthy guy," he replied, grinning. "And he wanted it as far away from Mexico City as possible."

"Why?" asked Jack, who didn't understand why Mr. Ortega didn't just put it away in a bank vault or inside a museum.

"Because he didn't want to be associated with it," he said. "He knew greedy people would hound him for it. And if he showed it to any of his fellow archaeologists, they would want to put it in a museum."

"What's wrong with that?" asked Jack. Museums, as far as he was concerned, were the best places for things like this.

"Well, because then the map would be on show!" he said. "It would be like a calling card to all treasure hunters: 'Come and see the map of Montezuma's gold!'"

Jack wasn't sure he agreed with Carlos Ortega's reasoning, but the fact was that someone had gotten their hands on the map. Jack figured he needed more information to find out who it could be.

"Is there anybody living in the house besides you?" asked Jack.

"No, just me," said Mr. Garcia. "My wife passed away many years ago."

"Does somebody help you clean your house?" asked Jack.

"Maria comes every other week," he said.

Jack thought this was interesting. Maybe this Maria had something to do with the theft. "Where does she live?" Jack asked.

"Two towns over," said the man. "But Maria is a very nice girl," he explained. "She would have had nothing to do with it."

"So where did you keep the map?" asked Jack. Although Mr. Garcia thought Maria was in the clear, Jack was keeping her in mind as a possible suspect.

"In a cookie jar in the kitchen," said the man.

Jack couldn't help but grimace. He couldn't believe something that precious had been kept in a cookie jar!

Seeing Jack's reaction, the man chimed in, "Seemed like the safest place to me! After all," he added, "who would keep something that important in a cookie jar?"

Exactly, thought Jack, but said aloud: "When did you notice it was missing?"

"This morning," Mr. Garcia replied, "when I got up to make my *café con leche*. I check the jar every day," he added, "and today the jar itself was gone."

"You did the right thing, calling the GPF," said Jack. "Mind if I take a look?" Jack wanted to see if there were any clues in the kitchen.

"By all means," said the old man.

Jack left Mr. Garcia and walked into the other room. As the man said, there was no cookie jar anywhere to be found. But there weren't any signs of forced entry—no broken windows or upturned furniture.

Returning to the den, Jack started to wonder if this old man was mad. Perhaps he had made the whole thing up.

"Do you remember what the map looks like?" asked Jack.

"I do," said the man. "I made a careful note of it in my brain."

Not sure whether the man's brain was all there, Jack figured he had no other choice but to try to pick it.

"Can you draw a picture of what you remember?" asked Jack.

The man grabbed a piece of paper and pen from his desk. As he started to doodle, he added, "You know, it was made from the flattened bark of a fig tree. It was very fragile."

Jack knew that the ancient Aztecs did use the bark of fig trees as paper. The fact that this man knew that told Jack that maybe he wasn't loony after all.

"Here you go," said the man, handing the piece of paper over to Jack.

As Jack looked down at the drawing, he

was amazed at what he saw. There before
him was a drawing of a possible treasure
map.

At the bottom was a picture of a horse with a long tail. Just above that was a picture of a building on top of a hill. Lastly, there was a picture of a triangular structure with a crescent moon on top.

Jack knew that the Aztecs used drawings instead of words to tell stories and count. Perhaps, thought Jack, they decided to use pictures to give the location of the buried treasure.

Jack knew something else about Aztec drawings. They placed things on top of one another to show distance. This meant the picture on the bottom was a possible starting point, with every picture on top farther away geographically.

But why were there several pictures, instead of just one? It would have been easier to give one clue to the location of the buried treasure. Maybe, Jack reasoned, there was a purpose in all of this. Perhaps there was something to see or collect at each place.

Jack figured one other thing too. Whoever had their hands on the map now was thinking the same. And given that they might have taken the map this morning, that meant they were at least a few hours ahead of Jack in locating the treasure.

Jack looked again at the first drawing. He thought it was curious that Mr. Garcia had drawn the horse's tail so long. "Was the horse's tail really this long?" asked Jack.

The old man nodded his head.

"Was there anything else unusual?" asked Jack. "Were the hairs on the tail thick, or perhaps painted a particular color?"

"Now that you mention it," said the man, "the horse's tail was blue. I thought that was pretty odd at the time, since most horsehairs are black or brown."

"Exactly," said Jack, who had an idea. Blue was the universally recognized color for water.

"Are there any waterfalls in Mexico where the water flows out like this?" asked Jack, pointing to the direction indicated by the tail.

"There's a waterfall east of here, in Monterrey," he offered. "Now you mention it, the water does flow in a similar arc."

"Perfect," said Jack, who was feeling confident at this new lead. "I'll find the map, and when I do, I'll make sure it comes back to you."

"Good luck on your journey," said Mr. Garcia.

"*Adios*," said Jack as he hurried out the door.

Chapter 6:
The Route

As soon as he left the old man's house, Jack pulled his Map Mate out of his bag. The GPF's Map Mate was a hand-held navigation device that gave you directions from one place to another, anywhere in the world.

What made the Map Mate so special was that it didn't need to have roads to guide you. It could give you directions over any type of terrain including jungles, deserts or even ice. The Map Mate always knew where you were and where you were going. All the agent had to do was follow the arrows.

After Jack programmed in the name "Monterrey," the Map Mate calculated Jack's route. According to the device, Jack needed to go eighty kilometers, or almost fifty miles, east. Looking around him, Jack couldn't see any public transport options and there was no way he could walk that far: he needed to get there fast!

Plucking his Flyboard out of his Book Bag, he placed the gadget on the ground. The GPF's Flyboard looked like a skate-board, only it used hydrogen-powered jets instead of feet to make it go. The Flyboard could carry an agent at a speed of twenty-five miles per hour as it hovered a yard off the ground.

Jack turned on the Flyboard by tapping

a few commands on his Watch Phone.
Once he'd strapped his Anti-detection
Visor over his eyes and Noggin Mold to his
head, he stepped on. Within moments,
Jack was moving east toward Monterrey
and possibly the first clue on the map.

Chapter 7:
The Forest

As Jack and the Flyboard entered the
area, he noticed that this part of Mexico
was greener than the land around Mr.
Garcia's house. It was also rugged, with
steep cliffs, mountains and canyons.

The arrow on the Map Mate was
flashing, telling Jack he was getting close.
It looked like he needed to find a route
through the small forest ahead.

When he reached the trees, he hopped

off the Flyboard and put away his protective gear. Ducking under some overgrown foliage, he stepped onto a muddy path. There, behind some leafy bushes was an old, wooden sign.

Although most of the sign's paint had been washed away, Jack could still make out a few words. It said, COLA DE CABALLO. Jack knew that meant "horse's tail" in Spanish. This was the path Jack was looking for.

He climbed the trail for about thirty yards, until he came to a clearing. There, in the middle of an open space, was a large pool of water. The pond was surrounded by a circle of rocks. The circle wasn't man-made; the rocks had been left by nature.

When the water in the pool got too high, it flowed over the rocks and down a steep hill. In doing so, it made a small waterfall that dropped below to another pool. But this wasn't the waterfall Jack was here to view. It was the one crashing from above, and it was absolutely beautiful.

As Jack craned his neck to see, the spray from the waterfall above sprinkled on his face. The water started from a narrow opening at the top of a cliff. As it poured out over the rocks in its way, it fanned out so that it looked just like the horse's tail in the drawing.

Sure that the picture of the horse must represent the waterfall, Jack thought about what to do next. He wondered whether the Aztecs had buried something important nearby. Or, whether the waterfall was the first part of a larger clue. Thinking that anything was possible, Jack started looking around.

He searched the side of the water that he was on, but he couldn't find a thing. There was nothing carved into any of the rocks, and nothing on any of the trees or bushes.

Knowing he had to get to the other side, Jack thought about his choices. He could walk over the rocks at the bottom edge, but one slip could send him tumbling down the next waterfall.

Or, he could swim across the pool itself. His clothes would eventually dry off, and his Book Bag and boots were waterproof. Jack climbed over one of the rocks and lowered himself into the chilly water. He was used to swimming in cool temperatures. What he wasn't used to was the feeling of something slimy swimming up his trousers.

Hoping it was a friendly fish rather than anything more dangerous, Jack continued to swim to the other side. Clambering over the rocks and onto dry land, Jack squeezed a bit of water out of his trousers and began to look around.

As he did, he saw something interesting. Behind the waterfall itself, he spied what looked like a cave. It had been hidden from view before, but now Jack could see it clearly. Shaking some water out of his ears, Jack made his way over to it.

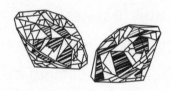

Chapter 8:
The Cave

As Jack approached the cave's entrance, he thought he could hear noises. Pulling away quickly, he stood with his back tight against the outside wall. Carefully, he craned his neck around the corner to see what was going on.

Inside the cave were five men. Four of them were stashing pickaxes and other tools into a burlap bag, while another man was giving orders.

"Hurry up!" shouted the leader. "We've got to get a move on if we're gonna find that gold!"

The others grunted and cackled with laughter. From what Jack could see, one or two of the men were missing their front teeth.

So, thought Jack, these were the guys. These were the men who had stolen the map from Mr. Garcia's house. Only thing was, he still couldn't figure out how they'd done it. Jack wondered whether they had already found something in the cave—something linked to Montezuma's treasure.

"Gather up that water too!" the leader yelled, still barking commands. "We've got a long day ahead. We're heading south." One of the men scurried to a corner of the cave and grabbed a few bottles.

So the mysterious men were heading

south, but where? Jack hadn't had a
chance to properly study the next clue on
the map.

Jack followed the bossy man with his
eyes. Until now, he'd had his back turned
to Jack, so he hadn't seen his face.

The man walked to the back of the
cave. There on the far wall was what
looked like a freshly made hole. The man

grabbed a knife from his hip pocket.
Using the tip, he picked a small red stone
out of the wall. It looked like a ruby. As it
came out of the wall, the stone fell into
his hand.

Placing the jewel in a small bag clipped
to his trousers, the man turned around
and returned to his men. As he did, Jack
got a good look at him.

The man was wearing red leather boots and dirty clothes. Above his right eye, he was missing an eyebrow.

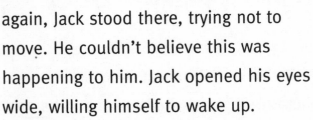

Throwing his back against the outside wall again, Jack stood there, trying not to move. He couldn't believe this was happening to him. Jack opened his eyes wide, willing himself to wake up.

But this wasn't a dream. The man in the cave was none other than Callous Carl, and the men with him were his gang of thieves.

Chapter 9:
The Dilemma

So now Jack knew who he was up against: one of the most dangerous treasure hunters that had ever lived! Jack needed to figure out how to catch these guys and bring them to justice.

He could burst into the cave and try to apprehend them. But his Book Bag didn't contain any gadgets that could overcome five guys at once. His Dozing Spray was only good for two people, and his Tornado only had ropes for binding up to three crooks. Plus, as strong and brave as Jack was, he was only a boy. There was no way he could physically overpower five grown men. It just wasn't going to happen.

Another idea was to call the local authorities. But Jack was in a remote location, and it would take the police a while to get there. Since Callous and his gang were about to move on, it would probably be too late. Making it even more difficult was the fact that Jack didn't know where they were off to. "South" wasn't enough of a lead.

The best thing, Jack figured, was to follow the gang, spy on them and gain more information. He scurried over to a leafy bush and crouched down behind it. Patience was the way to catch these guys, reasoned Jack. Patience, that is, and a lot of luck . . .

Chapter 10:
The Close Call

Just then, Jack heard some movement.
Callous Carl and his gang were leaving
the cave. They began walking out one by
one in a long line with Callous at the
back.

"Hurry up, you losers!" he yelled at his
men. Callous was definitely living up to
his name, thought Jack. He certainly
wasn't a warm and friendly guy.

As they passed by, Jack noticed what

they were carrying. The man in front was carrying the burlap bag of tools. The second was carrying the bottles and the third and fourth had packs strapped to their backs. Callous was carrying nothing but the small bag on his hip.

Jack reasoned that the red stone inside was somehow important to the treasure hunt. Otherwise, Callous wouldn't have bothered to take it from the cave. If Jack could get his hands on the bag or the jewel, he just might be able to stop Callous.

As the men approached the pool of water, one of them turned suddenly and started to march toward Jack! Crouching down, Jack tried to blend into a bush as best he could.

The man reached over him, and grabbed for a white rope that was lying on the other side. As he yanked, an inflatable boat came out of nowhere. It slid over Jack's head and onto the ground. Incredibly, the man hadn't seen Jack, because he carried on lugging the boat until he got to the edge of the water.

There, he placed it in the pool, and one by one the men climbed in. Using some thick sticks as oars, they paddled across the pond to the other side. When they reached it, they pulled the boat out of the

water. Callous took his knife out and slashed a hole in the side of the boat.

"That should stop anybody else from gettin' to the other side easily!" he grunted.

Leaving the remains of the boat behind, the men left the clearing and disappeared from view.

Now it was Jack's turn to make a move. He hurried out from behind the bush and quickly swam across the pond. Dripping when he came out, Jack shook himself off as best as he could. He left the waterfall and the pool behind and made his way down the trail the thieves had taken.

Chapter 11:
The Ride

Keeping a good distance between himself and the gang, Jack tried to listen in on what they were saying.

"What d'ya think we'll find at the next place?" called out one.

"Dunno," said another, "but I'm getting thirsty for gold!"

"Shut your traps!" growled Callous. "I told you to keep your mouths shut. We don't want anyone muscling in on our action."

The men grumbled in agreement.

This little conversation gave Jack an idea. He'd forgotten all about the second clue. If he could somehow get to the next location before Callous and his gang, then he could call the police and capture them before they went any further.

Quietly, Jack pulled out Mr. Garcia's drawing as he walked. The second clue was of a building at the top of a mountain.

As soon as he was in a stationary place, he could use his Double-A device to find the location.

Callous Carl and his gang stepped from the trail and onto the open road. Sticking close behind, Jack hid behind a tree as he watched. There, a few yards away, was a small truck. Hitched to the cab was a small trailer with a tarpaulin on top.

Callous was probably going to try and hide the treasure underneath the tarpaulin and smuggle it back to his headquarters. Jack, however, was thinking of a better, more immediate, use for the hiding place it provided.

As the men were climbing into the truck, Jack made a break for it. He ran from the forest and toward the trailer.

Lifting the tarpaulin, he crawled underneath. Within moments, the truck started up and the trailer began to roll. Callous and his men hadn't seen Jack. Now they were off to the next clue, with Jack going along for the ride.

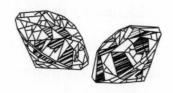

Chapter 12:
The Next Stop

Although it seemed risky, hiding in the
trailer was Jack's only choice. Since the
Torpedo was in for repairs, Jack didn't have
a gadget that could go more than twenty-
five miles per hour. Besides, Jack would
slip out when the truck slowed down.
Then, he could call the cops as Callous
and his men were at the next location.

In the meantime he had to figure out
where the truck was taking him. He pulled

out Mr. Garcia's drawing of the treasure map and looked hard at the building at the top of a mountain. Given that the Aztecs worshiped many gods, Jack wondered if this was some sort of religious temple.

Not wanting to move the tarpaulin too much, Jack wriggled as little as possible as he reached for his Double-A device. The two As were short for "Archaeology Assistant," and it was a necessary gadget for doing research on the ancient world.

All you had to do was type in a key word or phrase, and the Double-A device would feed back information about what you were looking for. Agents had used it on missions in ancient Greece, and now Jack was going to use it here in Mexico, to find out where they were headed.

After typing the words *temple*, *mountain*, and *south of Mexico City*, an entry popped up. There was a temple at the top of a mountain called Tepozteco. The mountain was just south of Mexico City.

Jack closed his eyes and allowed himself to nod off. After all, it would be hours before they got to the temple, and Jack needed to conserve his energy for the dangers ahead.

Chapter 13:
The Scare

THWACK!

CRUNCH!

Jack woke up suddenly—his body was being thrown around. The trailer had slowed to a crawl and was now jolting up and down.

Carefully lifting the tarpaulin's flap, Jack peeked out at the view. The truck was on a road in the middle of another forest. But this road wasn't made of tarmac, it was a dirt track, and there were large holes and rocks all over it.

Must be getting close to the temple, thought Jack. Time to slip out of the trailer.

Rolling his body over the back edge of the trailer, Jack let himself fall onto the bumper and then hit the ground.

Jack landed face-first in a muddy hole. Spitting out dirty water, he ran quietly into the bushes. The truck carried on until it came to a stop down the road.

Jack watched as Callous's men hopped out of the vehicle. They walked to the back of the trailer and lifted the cover. For a tense moment Jack wondered if they'd noticed he'd been there, because they stopped dead in their tracks. But then they carried on, taking some equipment and other bags with them.

"Hustle up!" said Callous Carl, stepping out of the truck in his red leather boots. "This is the second stop on the map. If y'all see anybody lurkin'," he said spitting on the ground, "kill 'em. And then ask questions later."

Jack gulped. Callous Carl meant business. He had no doubt that Callous had gotten rid of other people along the way. Now more than ever, it was important to be careful and clever.

The men disappeared into the forest and up a trail to the left. Crouching down,

Jack followed them closely. As the path rose steeply, the men grabbed sticks and vines to keep themselves anchored to the ground. Since Jack was smaller and lighter, all he needed were his hands and feet, which he used to scramble up the hill.

They'd climbed for nearly an hour when at last there was a break in the trees. From below, Jack watched as the men stepped over a ridge. Jack crawled toward it too.

It took him a few moments, but when he reached the top, he peeked over the ridge. There, on the top of the mountain, was a beautiful temple. Because of the difficult climb and its abandoned look, Jack reckoned no one had been there for many years. He saw the last man rush inside the building.

When Jack thought the area was clear,

he made his way over the ridge and onto
flat ground. He found a large boulder, and
perched himself against it.

This was the perfect moment, thought Jack. They were in a remote location and the gang was busy in the temple. All Jack had to do was summon the authorities and then they could surround the temple, trapping the crooks inside.

Pleased with his plan, Jack pushed a few buttons on his Watch Phone, ready to talk.

"*Hola,*" said a voice on the other end. It was the local police station.

"*Hola,*" said Jack, "*Habla inglés?*"

"Yes," said the voice on the other end. "What's your emergency?"

"There are five men," said Jack, "who are trying to steal—"

But before Jack could finish, a large shadow appeared before him. Out of nowhere, a knife swung in front of Jack's eyes and sliced his Watch Phone off his wrist. The gadget sailed into the trees and turned itself off, since it was no longer attached to Jack's arm.

When Jack looked down, he saw red leather boots. He gulped. He knew who it was. It was Callous Carl.

"What do you think you're doing?" the thief growled.

Jack got up and tried to run, but Callous grabbed him by his Book Bag and threw him to the ground.

"Oh, no you don't!" he seethed. "You're gonna pay for coming after me!"

Jack was on his back looking up. Callous held the knife's sharp blade between Jack's eyes. "I'm going to get you piece by piece!"

Jack's heart started to thump. He was finding it hard to breathe. The lack of air was making him dizzy.

"Boss!" yelled a voice in the distance.

Callous's eyes flicked away from Jack.

"Yeah?" He sneered in the direction of the voice. "What d'ya want?"

"We found it!" said the man.

Callous looked down at Jack. "I'm not finished with you, yet," he said. Talking to the man at the temple, he ordered, "Come over here and give me a hand with this kid."

The man rushed over.

"Tie him up!" barked Callous. He bent down close to Jack's face again and looked at him with evil eyes. "I'll come back for you when I'm done," he hissed.

The man did as Callous directed. Using a rope from behind his back, he quickly tied Jack's feet and hands together. Jack didn't dare do a thing. After all, if Jack tried to make a move, he had no doubt Callous would finish him off right then and there.

"That should do ya," grumbled the man. Then he and Callous went back inside the temple.

Chapter 14:
The Way Down

Jack wasn't sure what the men had found, but at this point he didn't much care. The most important thing was to get out of there—and fast.

He stared at his hands and feet. There was no way he could wriggle out of the ties. Hoisting himself into a sitting position, he reached his fingers down to his boots.

Mr. Davidson, the GPF tech wizard, had

stashed a few goodies in every secret agent's shoes. There was the Dome, an expandable bag, under the left sole. A Mine Alert feature was imbedded in the tips. Smoke-Screen Pellets were hidden in the right heel, while a miniature pocket knife was on the side of the left.

It was the last tool Jack was after. He moved his hands over the inside of that shoe and opened a small plastic door. Poking out was the top of the pocket knife. Taking it out, Jack immediately began to cut through the ropes.

Frantically, he looked at the temple doors. The last thing Jack needed was for Callous and his men to come out now. He carried on slicing until the ropes around his hands and his feet broke free.

Putting his knife back in his shoe, Jack quickly ran back to the path. But as soon as he did, he stopped. There was no way he could hike back down that trail. It was steep, and he guessed it would take at least forty-five minutes to descend.

The only other way off the mountain was to abseil. Abseiling was dangerous, and something the GPF recommended only in an emergency. Since Callous had threatened Jack's life and his hooligans were looting treasure, Jack figured this qualified as a critical time.

After pulling his Abseil Kit out of his Book Bag, he anchored the rope, slipped the harness around his waist and placed the Noggin Mold on his head. The floppy piece of rubber instantly hardened to form a protective shell.

Jack raced to the side of the mountain, and turned around with his heels on the edge. He was about to step backward when he heard a noise. It was coming from the temple. Callous and his men had discovered Jack was no longer there.

"The boy!" roared Callous. "He's escaped!"

Quickly, Jack lowered himself over the rim of the mountain, but not soon enough. One of the men noticed Jack's head popping up over the ridge.

"There he is!" he shouted. The men started running toward Jack.

Using his hands and feet as quickly as he could, Jack slid down the rope and the side of the cliff. As he dropped, he looked upward. Callous and his men were now

leaning over the side, watching Jack's every move.

"Get him!" shouted Callous.

ZING!

PING!

Jack ducked. A bullet ricocheted off a rock and into the trees. Only a few more moments and he'd be safe. The voice echoed again from above.

"Cut the rope!" Callous hollered.

Jack figured at least one of the men had a knife handy. He knew he didn't have much time. Moving quickly, Jack swung himself far to the right.

WOOSH!

The next thing Jack knew was that he was falling. One of Callous's thugs had cut the cord. Crashing into the treetops, his body bounced from branch to branch until it fell onto the ground with a thud.

As Jack lay there, he looked through the leaves. Callous and his men were still leaning over the ridge, checking that Jack was toast. He lay completely still to try and fool them.

From what Jack could see, the gang believed it. They stopped paying attention to Jack and stood up around Carl. Callous pulled something out of the bag on his hip, and as he lifted it to the sun Jack saw something blue sparkle. The gang let out a big cheer, and then Callous put the object away. Jack was pretty sure it was a stone like the one he'd seen at the cave, only this one was obviously a different color. The men congratulated themselves again, and then walked away from the side of the mountain.

Chapter 15:
The Ancient City

Gathering his throbbing body off the ground, Jack hid himself further under the foliage, so that he couldn't be seen. He put away the remnants of his gear and left his Noggin Mold on, just in case.

With no way to alert the authorities now that his Watch Phone was out of action, Jack was going to have to deal with matters himself. Pulling out Mr. Garcia's drawing, Jack took a look at the third and final clue.

The picture was of a triangular building with a crescent-shaped moon on top. It was pretty clear the building was a pyramid, but Jack couldn't figure out the significance of the moon.

Pulling out his Double-A Device, Jack typed the words *pyramid* and *moon*. Hundreds of entries came up, but one in particular caught Jack's eye:

The Pyramid of the Moon is located in the ancient Mexican city of Teotihuacán (say it like tay–o–tee–wah–kan). Archaeologists have discovered a series of underground tunnels there, although their purpose is still unknown. Approximate distance from present location: 100 miles northwest.

After reading the description, Jack had a strong hunch it was the right place. The fact that there were a group of underground tunnels pointed to a possibility of buried treasure.

If Jack was right, Callous and his men had already taken what they needed from the temple. Once they'd hiked back down the hill, they'd be off to the pyramid.

Pulling his Flyboard out, Jack snapped it together. He swiped his index finger over the identification grid, and soon the hydrogen jets were up and running. Jack took off northwest, his mind racing with how he would defeat Callous Carl. At least now he would have the element of surprise . . .

Chapter 16:
The Turning Point

Jack had been traveling for a few hours when he arrived at Teotihuacán, the ancient city that had thrived almost a thousand years ago. The ground was drier than it was down south, and there were scrubby bushes sticking out of it. The place seemed deserted, but Jack knew there were thieves lurking about.

Up ahead were several buildings. According to the Double-A device, one

was called the Pyramid of the Sun;
another was called the Temple of the
Feathered Serpent; and at the end of a
four-mile long road was the Pyramid of
the Moon. Jack and his Flyboard followed
the trail to this last temple.

Packing his gadget away, Jack began to search for clues. To the right of the building, he saw the back end of a vehicle. Jack recognized it as Callous's truck. But there wasn't anybody inside. Callous and his gang were probably already under the ground.

Perfect, thought Jack. In the four hours it took him to travel, Jack had hatched a new plan, found an old, dusty pay phone and made an important call. All Jack had to do now was lure the gang out of the cave, and his plan to trap them could be set in motion.

Chapter 17:
The Discovery

Jack found the entrance to the tunnels pretty quickly. Near Callous's truck was a sign sticking out of the dirt with the words KEEP OUT! On the ground next to it was a wooden panel with a handle. When Jack pulled the handle, he found himself staring down a hole in the ground.

Leading downward was a flight of steps. Holding the panel over his head open as long as he could, Jack headed into the depths. When he couldn't keep it open any longer, Jack let the wooden door close. At that moment, everything went dark.

Jack couldn't use his Everglo light, and he'd lost his Watch Phone in the forest. Instead, he used his hands to feel his way around. Counting the steps, Jack noticed there were twenty steps until he hit flat ground again. This must be the beginning of the tunnel, he thought, as he continued to move forward, trying to keep track of whether he was turning left or right. Eventually, up ahead, he could see a faint light. Figuring it was the treasure hunters, Jack made his way toward it.

As the light grew brighter, Jack could see what was up ahead. He was still in a long corridor, but the tunnel was opening into a large room. This room led to another, and so on and so on, until there was only one room left in the cavern.

It was in this last room that Jack found Callous and his band of thieves. They were staring at a painting on the back wall. The only light in the room was from an electric lantern, which was in the middle of the floor. Jack kept himself hidden in the doorway, so that he didn't announce his presence too soon.

The painting was of a man dressed in feathers. Recognizing the image immediately, Jack shuddered. It was of Quetzalcoatl—the feathered serpent—one of the most feared gods of the Aztec people.

But there was something odd about the figure. Whoever had painted it had left small round holes for the god's eyes. Seeing this made Jack think about the stones Callous had collected from the cave and the temple on the mountain. They looked to be the same size and shape as the eyes on the Aztec god.

Maybe, Jack reasoned, the first two clues on the map were about collecting the jewels. The third was about the place where you had to use them. Perhaps, Jack thought, if you placed the stones in the feathered serpent's eyes, it would reveal the location of the buried treasure.

Callous must have had the same thought too, because at that very moment he took the small bag from his hip. He reached inside and pulled out the blue stone. Lifting it to the wall, Callous stuck the jewel into one of the eyes. When he did, the wall swung forward a bit, revealing a secret chamber behind. From where Jack was standing, he could see something gold inside, sparkling in the light.

"The treasure's ours!" shouted Callous.

"Yahoo!" screamed the men, who were drooling and rubbing their hands.

Callous lifted the bag again. He was going to place the last stone in the wall when Jack decided to make a move.

Swooping in, Jack kicked the lantern across the floor, breaking it into pieces. Everything went completely black.

"What's happening?" screamed Callous

Carl. "What the heck happened to our light?"

Remembering where Callous was standing, Jack snatched the bag containing the red stone out of his hands. He turned and ran out of the room and into the tunnel.

"Somebody's stolen the bag!" yelled Callous. "Go after it!" he ordered his men.

Jack could hear the men fumbling around in the dark. Swiping his hands against the tunnel wall as he ran, Jack made sure he didn't crash into anything.

"Get him!" yelled Callous. "Turn another light on!" he screamed.

Jack kept racing toward the exit. He had to lure Callous's men out of the cave.

A light turned on behind Jack, but it wasn't soon enough. His foot jammed into the first step of the stairway and the bag flew out of his hands. Scurrying around, he found it again and started climbing the steps two at a time. The men were now entering the first room.

Reaching the top of the stairs, Jack flung the door open. Light poured into the cave. He dashed out and onto the ground. Jack looked around. But nobody was there.

Jack yelled out in frustration. He could hear Callous's goons stomping up the steps. In the distance, he noticed a small town. His only choice was to lead them there.

Sprinting as fast as he could, Jack headed onto the open plains. The men behind him were shouting vicious threats. They were slowly catching up to Jack.

In front of Jack was a prickly bush. Throwing his body over it, his feet came crashing to the ground. The men did the same. Jack could hear them grunt as they landed.

The next thing he knew, he heard the wheels of a car to his side. It sounded like it was churning up dirt. Thinking help had arrived, Jack was horrified to see that it was Callous driving the truck, with his gang of thieves just behind.

Then, out of nowhere, Jack tripped. He

fell forward to the ground, crashing onto his hands. Jack couldn't help but remember his nightmare. The events of it were exactly what was happening now.

The shadows of the men were closing in on Jack. As they reached for him, Jack screamed "No!"

Just then, Jack heard a horrible screeching sound. He wondered if Callous's car was out of control and headed for him. Jack looked toward the noise.

Speeding toward Jack were ten Mexican police cars, their sirens blaring loudly.

As soon as they saw the police, the men backed away from Jack. They started to run toward Callous and his truck, trying to flee the scene before being captured.

Callous slowed down to let the men climb in, but in doing so lost valuable

time. Nine of the police cars circled around the truck and surrounded the men. There was no way they could escape now.

The last car made its way over to Jack. It braked hard, sending dust spiraling into Jack's face. A Mexican officer hopped out. Knowing Jack was English, he spoke to him in his own language.

"Jack," he said, "I'm sorry we were late. I'd like to blame it on traffic," he added, smiling sheepishly, "but it's siesta time and I had a hard time waking my guys."

Jack shook his head. He didn't know whether to laugh or be angry.

"That's okay," said Jack. "In the end, you saved the day."

"No," said the officer. "It looks like *you* did. Callous Carl has been on the Most Wanted list for years. He's been terrorizing people and stealing treasure for as long as anybody can remember. With him locked up," he added, "Mexico will be a safer place."

Jack stood up and brushed the dust off his clothes. He handed the bag with the remaining stone to the officer.

"This needs to be protected," he said. "If you keep it safe, nobody will be able to steal Montezuma's gold."

"I'll hand it over to the proper authorities in Mexico City." said the officer.

"You'll also need to seal the site," said
Jack, "to make sure nobody else tries to
take anything from there."

"Already done," said the officer, "I've
sent some of my best men over to cover
it."

"Two more things," said Jack. "When you
search Callous, you'll find a map. When
you do," he explained, "you need to return
it to Mr. Garcia. This is his address." Jack
wrote it down on a piece of paper and
gave it to the man. "Tell him he needs to
put it in a safer place from now on." Jack
smiled.

Jack could tell the officer didn't completely understand, but he would probably do as Jack asked.

"Did you run a check on Maria, Mr.
Garcia's cleaner?" asked Jack.

"Sure did," said the officer. "That was a good hunch you had. One of Callous's men is related to her, which is how they knew about the map. We're sending officers to her house right now," he explained, "to pick her up and bring her in for questioning."

"Great," said Jack, who was pleased with how things were turning out.

As he looked over at Callous Carl, he couldn't help but smile. He was being dragged out of the truck, tossed to the ground and cuffed alongside his thugs. When the officers yanked Carl to his feet, the treasure hunter glared in Jack's direction.

"I'm going to get you," he mouthed to him.

"No, you won't," Jack mouthed back.

Carl growled, and then the officers shoved him and his goons into the back

of one of the squad cars. As the car drove away, Jack waved. It would be a long time before anyone saw Callous Carl again.

Chapter 18:
The Resolution

With everything sorting itself out, it was time for Jack to go. But, without his Watch Phone, he couldn't very well command it to transport him home.

He waited for the police to leave the scene and when he was sure everyone was gone, he opened his Book Bag. He pulled out his portable Magic Map and laid it on the ground. Whenever a secret agent was away from home, they could use this map and a piece from Whizzy to transport them to their mission.

But because Jack was trying to make the reverse happen, he had to do a very different thing. He placed his first finger over the country of England and counted to five. When it registered his fingerprint and his home destination, a light began to shine from within the country.

When it did, Jack yelled, "Off to England!" and the light burst, swallowing Jack into the map.

When he arrived, he found both he and his map standing in the middle of his room. He folded up his portable map and tucked his Book Bag back under his bed. Accessing the GPF secure site on his computer, he sent them an e-mail telling them of the mishap with his Watch Phone and asking for a new one. Then, he returned to his bed and opened his book about treasure hunters.

He flipped to the story about Callous Carl, and looked at the snarling face of that greedy man. Ripping the pages from his book, Jack crumpled them up and threw them in the wastebasket.

Callous Carl no longer existed, as far as Jack was concerned. Thanks to Jack, Carl was off the Most Wanted list. Carl was about to spend his days cleaning toilets, serving meals and washing clothes in a high-security prison. And that, thought Jack, was exactly where he deserved to be.

The Theft of the
Samurai Sword:
JAPAN
BOOK 11

Read the first
chapter here

Chapter 1:
The Madame

It was a hot summer night in a far away
country. A large lady wearing lots of
makeup and a pretty kimono was sitting
on top of a chair in the middle of a room.
Her ruby-red lips parted, and she spoke
to the four men standing before her. The
men were dressed in black from head to
toe. Hanging from their cheeks were black
veils. The only thing you could see was
their piercing dark eyes.

"OK, men," she said. "You've heard your instructions. Now go and claim my treasures."

The men bowed and shouted the word "hai" together. They held onto their batons, which were fixed to their sides, and then turned and ran out of the room.

Throwing her head back, the woman cackled with evil laughter. The glittery green powder that covered her eyelids sparkled in the light. As she brought her head forward, she smiled with smug satisfaction.

Now all Madame Midori had to do was sit back and relax. Within hours, her band of ninja thieves would return, bringing with them the treasures she so desperately wanted.